Robbie's Trail through Foster Care

Activity Book

Published by Robe Communications. Second edition, 2010. First edition, 2008.

ISBN: 978-1-935831-01-3

Printed in the United States of America

www.robbietherabbit.com

CONTENTS

A note to the grown-ups 4

1. What's in Your Control 5

2. The Trail through Foster Care 7

3. When Your Body Is Hopping Mad 9

4. Feeling Better when You're Upset 13

5. Sunshine Fairies 15

6. Speak Up! 21

7. What Is Going On?! 23

8. Who Do You Want to Be? 27

9. Sharing Your Feelings 33

A note to the grown-ups...

I'd like to extend a hearty "thank you" in advance for helping the special child in your life with some important life skills. As a former foster child and now a child welfare professional who helps others, I can assure you that you DO make a difference when you spend time with a child in care. When you choose to read to a child and help him work through activities such as these, you can help him better understand what's going on his life. And, trust me, that's huge.

If you bought this activity book online at Amazon.com, BarnesandNoble.com or at the site of some other book seller, you may not be aware that the activities in this book (ISBN: 978-1-935831-01-3) were designed to work hand in hand with two other Robbie Rabbit™ books:

ROBBIE'S TRAIL THROUGH FOSTER CARE ISBN: 978-1-935831-00-6

This engaging story is about Robbie Rabbit's journey into foster care. In this full-color book, Robbie is removed from his birthmother's home and placed with foster parents. Robbie meets his new foster family, learns what a foster kid is and experiences some commonplace behaviors as he adjusts to his new life. The ending is intentionally vague: Children don't know whether Robbie will end up with his mother or whether he'll ultimately be placed for adoption. Available supplemental materials include ROBBIE'S TRAIL THROUGH FOSTER CARE — ACTIVITY BOOK as well as ROBBIE'S TRAIL THROUGH FOSTER CARE — ADULT GUIDE (each of which are sold separately). Guaranteed best price at **www.robbietherabbit.com**.

ROBBIE'S TRAIL THROUGH FOSTER CARE — ADULT GUIDE ISBN: 978-1-935831-02-0

This companion piece, which provides background and tips for helping children in out-of-home care, exists primarily to help foster parents and child welfare professionals facilitate each activity in ROBBIE'S TRAIL THROUGH FOSTER CARE — ACTIVITY BOOK (sold separately). Instructions, talking points and answers (when applicable) are also included. Guaranteed best price at **www.robbietherabbit.com**.

Don't have these books yet? Get them. First, make sure you've read the ROBBIE'S TRAIL THROUGH FOSTER CARE story with the child. Then, read the first few pages of ROBBIE'S TRAIL THROUGH FOSTER CARE — ADULT GUIDE before you dive into ROBBIE'S TRAIL THROUGH FOSTER CARE — ACTIVITY BOOK with the child.

Please keep in mind that the activities in this book are designed to promote communication between a foster child and his caseworker, foster parents, therapist, CASA or other child welfare professional. Therefore, it's critical that the adult and child work *together* on these. Remember, the following exercises should never take the place of professional therapeutic intervention.

I hope you enjoy this special time with the foster child in your life.

Adam Robe, MSW

1. What's in Your Control

Circle each statement that IS in Robbie's control.

Robbie is going to a foster home.

Robbie takes his bunny and game to the Thompsons.

Another bunny took Robbie's toy.

Robbie felt angry at the bunny who took his toy.

Robbie yelled at the bunny who took his toy.

What Robbie thinks about

How Robbie acts

What Robbie reads

continued on next page

www.robbietherabbit.com

Circle each statement that IS in your control.

I live in (or will soon be going to) a foster home.

Someone at school says mean things to me.

What I think about

Getting my homework done

The words I say

The school I go to

I feel upset if someone spills milk on me during lunch.

When someone spills milk on me, I call that person a mean name and punch him.

I'm sad I can't live at home.

I tell someone when I'm feeling sad that I can't live at home.

2. The Trail through Foster Care

Why did Robbie have to go to a foster home?

_____

_____

What are some ways that other people take good care of you?
Circle each one that applies.

They make sure I have food.

They take care of me when I'm sick.

They give me hugs.

They listen when I talk.

They make sure I have clothes to wear.

They include me when they are talking to other people.

They take me places.

They are nice to me.

continued on next page

Can you think of a time when someone has not taken good care of you?

_____

_____

Why do you think you had to leave your home and go into foster care?

_____

_____

3. When Your Body Is Hopping Mad

When Robbie is angry, what does his body say? Write the answers on each blank.

continued on next page

Draw a picture of yourself being angry.

What makes you angry? _____

_____

_____

Is it OK to feel mad? _____

continued on next page

10

If Robbie does something wrong in any of the pictures below, draw an "X" on the picture.

Robbie kicks another bunny

Robbie hits another bunny

Another bunny takes Robbie's toy

Robbie yells at another bunny

11

This page left blank intentionally.

4. Feeling Better when You're Upset

Hopping Mad and Feeling Bad

Shut those eyes;

Give three big sighs;

Walk away;

Come back to say, "Hey... let's talk."

www.robbietherabbit.com

This page left blank intentionally.

5. Sunshine Fairies

Who are the people in your life?

My friends are: _____

_____

I live with: _____

_____

I used to live with: _____

_____

Some other people in my life are: _____

_____

_____

continued on next page

Who are Robbie's sunshine fairies? Circle the animals that are most like sunshine fairies.

Tony

Rita

Jamie

Papa

therapist

Sammy

Who are your sunshine fairies?

_____

_____

continued on next page

Sunshine Fairy playing cards

Teacher	Doctor
Mom	Dad
Brother	Sister
Caseworker	Grandpa
Grandma	Aunt

This page left blank intentionally.

Your CASA

Your guardian ad litem

Uncle

A friend's mom

A friend's dad

Your favorite superhero

Your favorite princess

Your therapist

Your best friend

A neighbor

This page left blank intentionally.

6. Speak Up!

What can you do if you feel lonely? Circle two ideas that you like.

Cry.

Tell your foster parents that you feel lonely. Ask them if they'd like to play a game with you.

Tell your foster parents that you feel lonely. If you miss your old friends, ask your foster parents if your old friends can play with you sometime.

Tell one of your sunshine fairies how you feel.

Tell your teacher that you're lonely. Ask if she can help you make some new friends at school.

What can you do if you feel sad? Circle two ideas that you like.

Tell your foster parents that you feel sad. Ask them if you can have a hug.

Tell one of your sunshine fairies how you feel.

Crawl into bed and hide under the covers.

Color a pretty picture.

continued on next page

What can you do if someone is mean to you at school? Circle two ideas that you like.

Cry.

Hit the other person in the nose.

Take three deep breaths while you decide what you're going to do.

Say to the other kid: "You're not fun to play with when you act that way." Then walk away and find someone else to play with.

Tell a teacher that you feel bad because some of the children aren't being very nice to you.

7. What Is Going On?!

Circle what's different in Robbie's life.

Robbie had to leave his mom.

Robbie had to move into a house with strangers.

Robbie was served food that he's never seen before (hogwash soup).

Robbie looks different.

Robbie must go to a new school.

Robbie sees kids at school that he's never seen before.

Robbie must go to a new daycare.

Robbie isn't a bunny anymore.

Robbie doesn't live down the street from his friend Timmy anymore.

continued on next page

www.robbietherabbit.com

Circle what's different in your life. Then circle the faces that show how you feel about these changes.

I had to leave my mom when I moved to a foster home.

sad   angry   confused   scared   worried   happy   OK

I had to leave my dad when I moved to a foster home.

sad   angry   confused   scared   worried   happy   OK

I had to leave my home.

sad   angry   confused   scared   worried   happy   OK

I've been served food that we've never had at my house before.

sad   angry   confused   scared   worried   happy   OK

continued on next page

I must go to a new school.

sad angry confused scared worried happy OK

I see kids at school who I've never seen before.

sad angry confused scared worried happy OK

I must go to a new daycare or someplace new after school.

sad angry confused scared worried happy OK

I don't live near my old friends anymore.

sad angry confused scared worried happy OK

continued on next page

I share a room with someone now.

I don't share a room anymore with anyone.

There are other kids living in the house now besides me. (At my house, I was the only kid there.)

There aren't other kids living in the house now — there's just me. (At my house, I wasn't the only kid there.)

8. Who Do You Want to Be?

What kind of person are you? Think of five words that describe you.

1. _____

2. _____

3. _____

4. _____

5. _____

What is your favorite thing about yourself?

_____

Do you like the person you are?

_____

continued on next page

Who do you want to be?

1. _____

2. _____

3. _____

4. _____

5. _____

6. _____

7. _____

8. _____

9. _____

10. _____

"Me" playing cards

Happy	Sad
Calm	Worried
Have several good friends	Don't have any good friends
Good friend to others	Mean to others
Cheerful	Grumpy

This page left blank intentionally.

Patient	Always in a hurry
Laugh a lot	Angry
Honest	Not trusted by other people
Healthy	Sick or tired a lot
Help other people	Lonely

This page left blank intentionally.

9. Sharing Your Feelings

What is Robbie feeling in each of these pictures? Circle your answers.

I think Robbie feels:

upset   confused   angry   worried
scared   relieved   sad   happy

What can I do when I feel this way?

_____

_____

I think Robbie feels:

upset   confused   angry   worried
scared   relieved   sad   happy

What could Robbie do if he's feeling nervous or scared about meeting Rita? _____

_____

continued on next page

What is Robbie feeling in each of these pictures? Circle your answers.

I think Robbie feels:

excited   loved   happy   relieved

surprised   nervous   upset   angry

If Robbie is excited or happy, should he tell Rita how he's feeling? _____

_____

I think Robbie feels:

upset   confused   angry   worried

scared   lonely   sad   embarrassed

If Robbie feels bad about what the snake said, what should he do? _____

_____

CPSIA information can be obtained
at www.ICGtesting.com
Printed in the USA
264796LV00002B